SORRY, I Forgot to Ask!

BEST ME
I Can Be

Written by
Julia Cook

Illustrated by
Kelsey De Weerd

BOYS TOWN Press
Boys Town, Nebraska

*For everyone who
forgets to ask
~ Julia*

SORRY, I Forgot to Ask!
Text and Illustrations Copyright © 2012, by Father Flanagan's Boys' Home
ISBN: 978-1-934490-28-0

Published by the Boys Town Press
13603 Flanagan Blvd.
Boys Town, NE 68010

For a Boys Town Press catalog, call **1-800-282-6657**
or visit our website: **BoysTownPress.org**

Publisher's Cataloging-in-Publication Data

Cook, Julia, 1964-

Sorry, I forgot to ask! : my story about asking for permission and making an
apology! / written by Julia Cook ; illustrated by Kelsey De Weerd. -- Boys Town, NE :
Boys Town Press, c2012.

p. ; cm.
(Best me I can be ; 3rd)

ISBN: 978-1-934490-28-0

Audience: grades K-6.
Summary: Shows readers how to do a better job of asking for permission,
and making an apology. RJ learns that using these skills means a lot fewer
trips to the "time-out" chair.

1. Children--Life skills guides--Juvenile fiction. 2. Apologizing--Juvenile fiction.
3. Thought and thinking--Juvenile fiction. 4. [Success--Fiction. 5. Apologizing--
Fiction. 6. Thought and thinking--Fiction.] I. De Weerd, Kelsey. II. Series:
Best me I can be (Boys Town) ; no. 3.

PZ7.C76984 S67 2012

E   1202

Printed in the United States
10 9 8 7

Boys Town Press is the publishing division
of Boys Town, a national organization
serving children and families.

My name is RJ,
and I'm in my "Time to Think
about It" chair again.

I've been in this chair
a lot lately.

Friday after school,
my best friend Sam and I decided
we didn't want to ride the bus,
so we walked home instead.

On the way home, we had
a rock-throwing contest in the field.

We took our shoes off and went wading in the frog pond –
but we didn't catch any frogs.

Then, we stopped at the
corner store and bought slushies.

I got bubblegum blueberry
and Sam got grape.

When I walked into my house, my mom looked worried. She smiled and ran over and gave me a great big hug.

"RJ – I was so worried about you! Where have you been?"

"Well, Sam and I decided that we didn't want to ride the bus so..."

"You walked home?"

"Yes, and on the way home we had a rock throwing con..."

"RJ! You can't just decide not to take the bus!
You have to ask for permission!
We just spent the last two hours looking for you!

Sam's mom and dad
were worried.

Your teacher was worried.
The bus driver was worried.

And your dad and I
were worried sick!"

7

"But why are you so upset? All we did was walk home."

"RJ, I'm upset because you didn't ask for permission
and we didn't know where you were."

"Sorry, I forgot to ask."

"Sometimes saying 'sorry'
just isn't enough."

Why don't you go sit on
the 'Time to Think about It'
chair for a while."

On Saturday morning, Sam was over at my house
   and we were playing video games.
   We needed to get a code off of the Internet to win the game.

   My parents always make me ask for permission
before I get on the Internet, but my dad was outside washing the car
   and my mom was on the phone talking to my Aunt Sylvia.

"Just get on real quick
     and look it up," Sam said.

   We went into my dad's office
and logged on to the computer...
     just as my mom got off the phone.

"RJ!" she said.
"You know you have to ask for permission
before you get on the Internet."

"We were just looking up a game code.
What's the big deal?"

"The deal is you know the rule
and you broke the rule.

Sam, please go home. RJ…"

"I know, I know...
I need to go sit some more."

That afternoon, when my little sister Blanche and I got back from our piano lessons, we walked into the house and it smelled like a cup of hot chocolate!

Dear RJ & Blanche,
I'm picking up Grandma.
I'll be home in 10 minutes.
Your snack is on the table.
Love, Mom

My mom had made her ultimate famous triple-layer double-chocolate cake with whipped cream frosting! There it was... sitting right on the counter.

14

Next to the cake
was a note:

Dear RJ & Blanche,
I'm picking up Grandma.
I'll be home in 10 minutes.
Your snack is on the table.
Love, Mom

I looked over at the table:
	apples, string cheese, and graham crackers.

"I don't want to eat this stuff," said Blanche. "I want cake!"

"Me too!"

	"Should we wait to ask Mom?"

"Well, if we just eat a tiny piece,
      she probably won't even notice."

We both ate a tiny, little piece.

It tasted SOOOO good!
Then, we each had another tiny piece...
            and another...
                  and another...

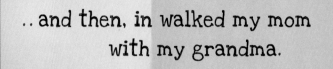

.. and then, in walked my mom
with my grandma.

At first, my mom smiled,
but when she saw us eating the cake
she got tears in her eyes and her face turned sad.

"RJ and Blanche," she said. "You ate the cake!"

"Yeah and it's SOOOO good!" I said.

"That was Grandma's special birthday cake."

"I told you we should have asked, RJ," Blanche said.

"Uh oh... Sorry."

19

"Both of you need to spend some time thinking about what you just did."

"I know... I know..." I said. "Back to the chair... come on, Blanche... let's go."

About 16 YEARS LATER, my dad came over and we had a talk.

"RJ, you are really struggling lately with asking for permission.

You walked home from school without asking.
You got on the Internet without asking.
And, you helped yourself to Grandma's special birthday cake
without asking and spoiled Mom's party plans.

I know you
can do better."

"When you ask for permission, you should:"

*LOOK right at the person
when you're ready to ask.*

*Use a CALM, pleasant voice,
and don't talk too fast.*

*ASK "May I please . . . "
and then do your best*

*to STAY CALM if the
answer is a NO or a YES.*

"Yeah, but when I remember to ask,
the answer is usually 'NO, RJ.'"

"Just keep asking...
The better you are at accepting 'NO' the right way,
the more likely we'll say 'YES' the next time."

I felt really bad about eating my Grandma's birthday cake,
but I didn't know what to say to her.

Mom went to the store and bought another chocolate cake
for the party, but it just wasn't the same.

On Monday, when I got back to school, Sam and I got sent to the principal's office.

"RJ and Sam," he said. "You both had everybody really worried on Friday. You can't just decide on your own that you want to walk home from school... you have to ask for permission.

Now you need to apologize, and just saying the word 'sorry' is not enough."

"What do I say?" I asked.

"To say you're sorry, you should:"

LOOK right at the person,
you've got nothing to fear.

Say "I'M SORRY" or "I apologize for..."
You must be sincere.

Explain your NEW PLAN
to be the best you can be.

Then finish by saying,
"THANKS for listening to me."

My principal showed both me and Sam how to apologize the right way. Then we had to practice doing it like 100 times!

After that, we told our teacher and the bus driver how sorry we were. I made so many apologies, that I was actually getting pretty good at it!

When I got home from School,
     I asked my mom to take me over to my grandma's
   So I could apologize – the right way – for eating her cake.

I realized that asking for forgiveness is a lot harder
than just asking for permission in the first place.

My grandma loved my apology. She gave me a great big hug.

The next Saturday, Grandma and I made an ultimate
famous triple-layer double-chocolate cake
with whipped cream frosting,
and we gave it to my mom.

Tips for Parents and Educators

JULIA COOK

Because Kids Don't Come With Instructions.

- Give children reasons why asking for permission and making sincere apologies are necessary skills they need to learn and use. Reasons could include: Asking adults for permission makes it more likely they will say "Yes" now or later and helps kids stay out of trouble. Making apologies helps maintain good friendships, helps others forgive the mistake, and makes it less likely they will carry a grudge or stay mad. (For example, say to children: "Asking me for permission will keep you out of trouble, and the more often you ask, the better the chance of me saying 'Yes.'" "Making apologies can help you become a better friend, and help others forgive you when you make a mistake.")

- Teach children to accept responsibility for their own behavior and actions. (For example, don't accept statements such as "the milk spilled," instead, encourage the child to say "I spilled the milk.") Help children learn to admit to their mistakes as opposed to finding fault with others or making excuses for their behavior.

- Make a conscious effort to model the social skills by finding ways to ask children for their permission. ("May I please use your pen?") Also genuinely say you are sorry when you make a mistake or do something you regret.

- Thank/recognize children when they ask you for permission, ("Thanks for asking...")

- Teach young children that their actions affect others. ("If you pull on a cat's tail, it will hurt and the cat will cry. If you pet him nicely, the cat will purr.")

- Explain to children that "being sorry" is an action, not just an expression. Sometimes saying they are sorry won't be enough to rebuild trust or fix a problem. Teach children to make amends by saying they are sorry, admitting to what they have done wrong, and then help them come up with a plan to either correct the problem or prevent the same mistake again.

- When a child breaks a rule, have consistent consequences for that child. Children need to know where the line in the sand is, and what will happen to them if they choose to cross that line. When their misbehavior or rule breaking has hurt someone or disrupted the home or classroom, they must learn that making an apology is necessary before they can resume normal activities or regain privileges.

For more parenting information, visit boystown.org/parenting.

BOYS TOWN®
Saving Children Healing Families

Boys Town Press Books by Julia Cook

Kid-friendly titles to teach social skills

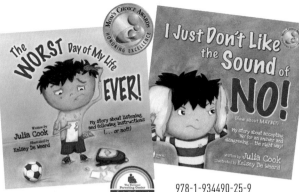

978-1-934490-20-4
978-1-934490-34-1 (SPANISH)

978-1-934490-25-9
978-1-934490-53-2 (SPANISH)

This series empowers kids with the skills and grit to grow their patience muscles, use flexible thinking, and become their best selves!

Reinforce the social skills RJ learns in each book by ordering its corresponding teacher's activity guide and skill posters.

978-1-944882-93-8

Wait-My-Turn Squishy
Available at BoysTownPress.org!

978-1-934490-28-0

978-1-934490-35-8

978-1-934490-43-3

978-1-934490-49-5

978-1-934490-67-9

The LEADER I'll Be!

A book series that teaches children how to use collaboration, creativity, and compromise to influence others.

It's My Way or the Highway
The Great Compromise
The I in Integrity
Good Things Come to Those Who Wait

Socially Skilled Kids

A book series celebrating unique kids who need support tackling shyness, following instructions, bedtime routines, and more!

Herman Jiggle, Go to Sleep!
Herman Jiggle, Say Hello!
Herman Jiggle, It's Recess Not Restress!
Herman Jiggle, Just Be You!

Building RELATIONSHIPS

A book series to help kids get along.

Making Friends Is an Art!
Cliques Just Don't Make Cents
Tease Monster
Peer Pressure Gauge
Hygiene...You Stink!
I Want to Be the Only Dog
The Judgmental Flower
Table Talk
Rumor Has It...

COMMUNICATE with Confidence

A book series to help kids master the art of communicating.

Well, I Can Top That!
Decibella and Her 6-Inch Voice
Gas Happens!
The Technology Tail

Responsible ME!

A book series to help kids take responsibility for their behaviors.

But It's Not My Fault
Baditude!
The PROcrastinator
Cheaters Never Prosper
That Rule Doesn't Apply to Me!
What's in It for Me?

BoysTownPress.org

For information on Boys Town, its Education Model®, Common Sense Parenting®, and training programs:
boystowntraining.org | boystown.org/parenting
training@BoysTown.org | 1-800-545-5771

For parenting and educational books and other resources:
BoysTownPress.org
btpress@BoysTown.org | 1-800-282-6657